BIG TIME
AUDITION

Adapted by Alana Cohen

Based on the episodes "Big Time Audition-Parts 1 and 2"
Written By Scott Fellows

Based on the Television Series "Big Time Rush"
Created By Scott Fellows

SCHOLASTIC INC.

New York   Toronto   London   Auckland
Sydney   Mexico City   New Delhi   Hong Kong

nickelodeon

BIG TIME RUSH

ISBN 978-0-545-35845-3

Published by Scholastic Inc.
SCHOLASTIC and associated logos are trademarks and/or registered trademarks of Scholastic Inc.

12 11 10 9 8 7 6 5 4 3 2 1   11 12 13 14 15/0

Printed in the U.S.A.   40
First printing, September 2011

Four friends named Kendall, Carlos, Logan, and James stood outside after school. They were talking about pulling a prank on the girls' field hockey team.

Kendall was really excited. "An opportunity like this comes once in a lifetime! We have to make the most of it!" he said with a big smile.

But James wasn't paying attention. He combed his hair. "I had my pop star dream again last night. I wore my lucky white T-shirt and I sang a cool song," he said. His friends were staring at him. "Oh . . . what are we doing?"

"We are going to soak the girls' field hockey team," Kendall explained.

The friends turned on the sprinkler. Then they saw a gush of water spray the field. Seconds later, they heard the girls screaming.

"And now we run," Kendall said as he saw the girls rushing toward them.

After barely escaping the field hockey team, the guys hung out at Kendall's house.

Then an announcement came on television: "Gustavo Rocque, a huge music producer, is looking for his next pop superstar in Minnesota. Sign ups are until five PM."

James couldn't believe it! His dreams of becoming a pop star were going to come true!

The friends had to get to the theater so that James could sign up. It was already four-thirty. They only had a half hour to get there.

The guys pulled up at the theater one minute before five o'clock. They were just in time! In the lobby, James introduced himself to Kelly, Gustavo's assistant.

"My name is James Diamond and I want to be famous," he said proudly.

Kelly placed a sticker with the number "810" on his shirt. Then she said, "Wait for your number to be called."

The other guys cheered. They were glad that James got to sign up!

Then Kelly looked at Logan. "What's your name?" she asked. Logan wasn't interested in auditioning. "Me? Oh, no thank you," he said. "I'm going to be a doctor."

But Kelly wanted Logan to sing for Gustavo anyway. She thought that he had pop star potential.

"I want to be famous, too!" Carlos said.
He sang for Kelly. Then he got a number.

Next Kelly looked at Kendall and asked, "Do you want your dreams to come true today?"

"Sorry," Kendall replied. "My dream is to become a professional hockey player."

Kelly smiled. Then she gave Kendall a sticker. She looked at James and said, "Number 810 is next."

James was very nervous. He switched numbers with Logan so that he wouldn't have to go yet. "You're next!" James said to Logan.

Logan stood on the stage in the audition room. He started to beat box, "zzzzip bop-bacha-bacha-bakah-zzzzp-zuuuup-wha-cha-ca-wow . . ."

But after a few moments, Gustavo stopped Logan. Gustavo yelled and said some things that weren't very nice.

Logan ran out of the room and joined his friends in the lobby. "Don't go in there!" Logan warned. "He is a very mean man!"

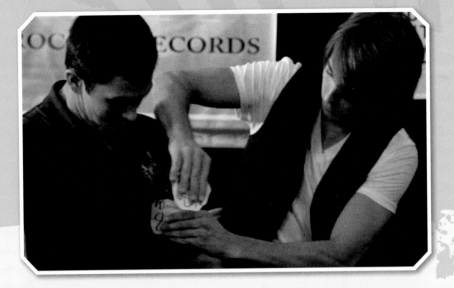

"811 is up!" Kelly called out.

It was James' turn. He quickly switched stickers with Carlos.

"All you, buddy! Go for it!" he said.

Carlos looked over at Logan and saw how upset he was. So he decided to make a joke out of his audition. He went on the stage and danced.

Then he burped into the microphone! This made Gustavo very angry.

It was time for James to audition. He was still nervous. So he tried to switch numbers with Kendall, but Kendall stopped him.

"This is your dream, not mine. Now grab on to that dream with both hands and go big time!" Kendall said. He pushed James into the audition room.

James went on the stage and started to sing. He sounded great! But then he noticed Gustavo's mean look. James got scared, and his voice cracked.

Gustavo told James to stop singing. "You have no talent!" Gustavo yelled.

James' friends had snuck into the room to hear his audition. Kendall didn't like how Gustavo treated his friend.

He jumped onto a table in front of Gustavo. "No talent?" shouted Kendall. "You're the one with no talent!" Then he made fun of a song Gustavo had produced.

Even though Kendall was just trying to be funny, his singing and dancing were really good! Then he did a dance move that knocked Gustavo off his chair. Gustavo turned bright red.

The guys were about to be in big time trouble. They ran out of the theater as fast as they could!

The guys went back to Kendall's house. They told Kendall's mom about the audition.

Then the doorbell rang. When Kendall opened the door, Gustavo and Kelly were standing outside.

James gave Gustavo a hug. "I knew you'd come back to me!" he said.

Gustavo pointed at Kendall. "I'm not here for you. I'm here for him."

"What?" all four friends asked with confusion.

Kendall's mom invited Gustavo and Kelly inside. Gustavo explained that he wanted Kendall to record songs in Los Angeles.

"But I'm not a singer," Kendall insisted.

"You sing all the time," said Katie, Kendall's little sister. "In the car, at the table, when you shovel the driveway . . ."

Kendall still didn't think that he should be a pop star. "I'm not interested," he said.

Gustavo was very angry that Kendall didn't want to sing. He stormed out of the house.

Before Kelly left, she gave Kendall her business card. "Call me if you change your mind," she said. "We leave tomorrow afternoon."

The next day, Carlos, James, and Logan went to the market to visit Kendall at work. The three friends asked Kendall why he turned down Gustavo's offer.

"I don't want to go to Los Angeles," Kendall said. "I want to be here with you guys and play hockey."

"But think about California. It has the beach, the stars, and best of all, the girls!" Carlos said.

"None of that matters if my best friends aren't there," Kendall replied.

James wished that Gustavo chose him instead. But he still wanted the best for his friend. "You should call that guy back. Opportunities like this come once in a lifetime."

"So if you all had a chance to go to Los Angeles to record songs with a big mean producer, you would go?" Kendall asked his friends.

"Yes!" they replied.

Kendall called Kelly and told her that he changed his mind. Soon, Gustavo and Kelly's limo arrived at the parking lot outside the market.

"I will go to Los Angeles with you to record some songs . . . *if* you take my buddies and make us a singing *group*," Kendall told Gustavo.

"I have toured twenty-two cities and haven't been able to find my next star. But I'm not desperate. There is no way I'm taking the four of you to Los Angeles."

Kendall knew Gustavo was lying. "So, we have a deal?" he asked.

"Yep," answered Gustavo.

A week later, the four friends, Katie, and
Kendall's mom arrived in Los Angeles. It
was warm and sunny. "We are *so* not in
Minnesota anymore!" Logan said.